D1123726

THE NINJA CLUB SLEEPOVER

For Kimberly, my fabulous, fierce friend.
—L. G.

To my family and friends,
for always encouraging me to be myself.
—M. H.

First published in 2020 by Page Street Kids
an imprint of
Page Street Publishing Co.
27 Congress Street, Suite 105
Salem, MA 01970
www.pagestreetpublishing.com

Distributed by Macmillan, sales in Canada by The Canadian Manda Group

20 21 22 23 24 CCO 5 4 3 2 1
ISBN-13: 978-1-62414-940-5 ISBN-10: 1-62414-940-5
CIP data for this book is available from the Library of Congress.

This book was typeset in Merge. The illustrations were done digitally.
Printed and bound in Shenzhen, Guangdong, China

Page Street Publishing uses only materials from suppliers who are committed to responsible and sustainable forest management.

Page Street Publishing protects our planet by donating to nonprofits like The Trustees, which focuses on local land conservation.

THE NINJA CLUB SLEEPOVER

LAURA GEHL

ILLUSTRATED BY MACKENZIE HALEY

Willa, Fiona, and Val played Ninja Club every day at school, chanting at the tops of their lungs:

"WE ARE NINJAS, AND NINJAS ARE BRAVE!"

Willa and her friends had matching ninja backpacks. They had matching ninja T-shirts. For a while, they even had matching ninja tattoos.

Now Val was hosting a Ninja Club sleepover for her birthday! It would be Willa's very first sleepover.

But Willa knew she was different from her friends.

Very different.

Underneath her ninja T-shirt, Willa's heart held a deep, dark secret. And Val's birthday was on a night with a full moon.

At home, Willa sulked.

"I hate being a **werewolf**," she said, scowling. "When the moon comes out, I'll turn into a scary, ugly monster. And scary, ugly monsters don't have any friends."

"There's nothing wrong with being a werewolf," Mom said. "Are you sure you're not just nervous about your first sleepover?"

"NO!" Willa said. **"I AM A NINJA, AND NINJAS ARE BRAVE!** But . . . ninjas don't have fur. Ninjas don't have claws. And ninjas *never* howl at the moon."

"Your friends will understand," Mom said.

No way, Willa thought. Nobody would understand a furry, howling ninja—not even her two best friends.

So she came up with a plan: *If the moonlight never hits my skin, then I won't change into a stinky old wolf.*

The night of the sleepover, Willa, Fiona, and Val cut out ninja swords,

made ninja masks,

and baked ninja cupcakes.

Willa could only eat one bite. The thought of going out into the moonlight made her tummy feel like tiny ninjas were tumbling inside.

"Time for the obstacle course," Val declared.

Willa glanced back at the moon. "We need to put on our ninja gear first!"

She made her way toward Val's bedroom.
Carefully.

When Willa reached the room . . .

she dove under a blanket to hide from the moon.

Val giggled. “Willa, we’re the Ninja Club, not the Ghost Club.”

Even with her skin covered, Willa didn't want to go out into the moonlight.

*I AM A **NINJA**, AND NINJAS ARE **BRAVE**,* she reminded herself.

"READY!"

tside, the three brave ninjas
d, swung, and climbed.

Until . . . Fiona fell.

“Are you okay?” Willa asked. “It looks like you landed on something.”

“I’m fine,” Fiona yelped, trying to move into the shadows.

But it was too late.

"You're a fairy?" Val exclaimed.

Fiona started to cry. "There's no such thing as a fairy ninja. Ninjas don't drink nectar. Ninjas don't love dancing. And ninjas *never* have wings!"

Val and Willa stared at Fiona's beautiful wings sparkling in the moonlight.

Then Willa's gaze returned to Fiona's tear-stained face.

"Who says ninjas don't have wings?" Willa asked. "Fairies are strong. Fairies are fast. Fairy ninjas are awesome!"

"I just want to be a normal ninja like you guys," Fiona sniffled.

Thoughts tumbled back and forth in Willa's head like two battling ninjas.

Should I tell Fiona?

NO! *Then she'll be scared of me.*

It might make her feel better . . .

NO! *She'll want to fly away!*

"I AM A NINJA, AND NINJAS ARE BRAVE!" Willa whispered.

She took a deep breath and pulled off her gear.

The moonlight hit Willa's skin.

"How about a **werewolf** ninja?" Willa asked. "Is that a 'normal' ninja?"

Fiona took a huge step backwards.

And another.

And another.

Val's wide eyes looked like two full moons. Willa's heart sank.

"It's still me," Willa said, her words coming out low and growly.

There was silence for a moment.

Then Fiona spoke softly. "You know, claws could be good for a ninja."

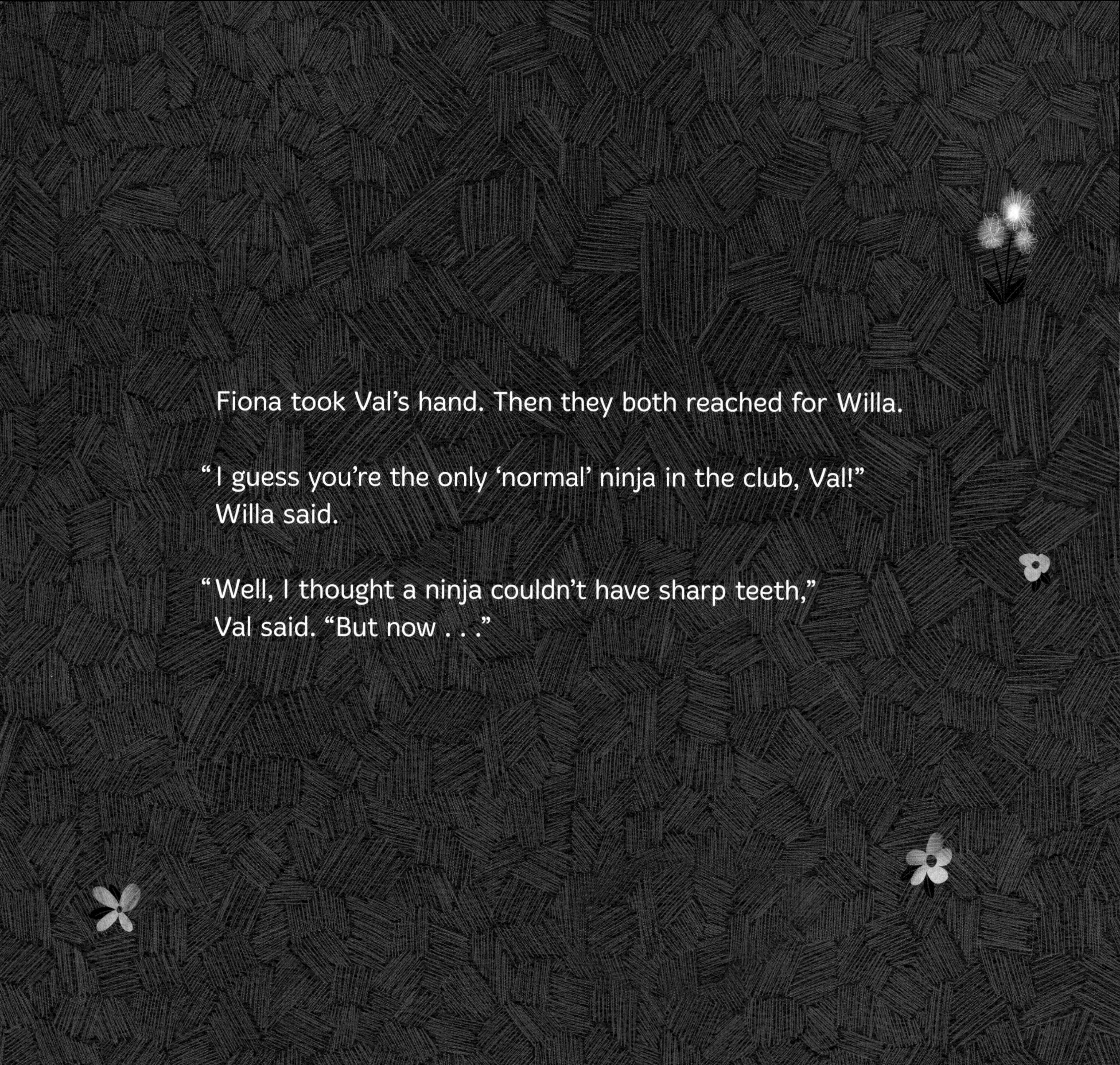

Fiona took Val's hand. Then they both reached for Willa.

"I guess you're the only 'normal' ninja in the club, Val!" Willa said.

"Well, I thought a ninja couldn't have sharp teeth," Val said. "But now . . ."

Val pulled down her scarf.

Fiona gasped, then grinned.
"A **werewolf**, a fairy, and a **vampire**? We're the weirdest ninja club ever."

"We're the **BEST** ninja club ever," Willa said. "And this is the **BEST** sleepover ever!"

"Speaking of sleep," Val said, "is it okay if we leave a light on when we go to bed? I'm kinda scared of the dark."

"And I'm a teeny bit scared to sleep away from home," Willa said.

"Me too," Fiona admitted.

"We will help each other be brave!" Val proclaimed.

"Ninjas forever!" Fiona added.

"AROOOOOO!" Willa howled.

Then the three friends chanted together at the tops of their lungs,

"WE ARE NINJAS, AND NINJAS ARE BRAVE!"

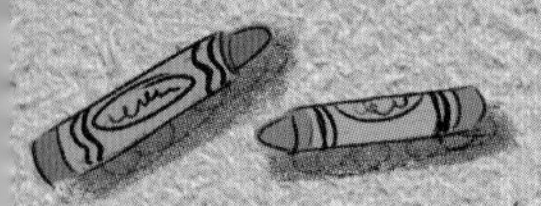